D1180637

C334234391

LITTLE TIGER PRESS LTD,
an imprint of the Little Tiger Group
1 Coda Studios, 189 Munster Road, London SW6 6AW
www.littletiger.co.uk

First published in Great Britain 2018
Text and illustrations copyright © Jane Chapman 2018
Visit Jane Chapman at www.ChapmanandWarnes.com

Jane Chapman has asserted her right to be identified as the author and illustrator
of this work under the Copyright, Designs and Patents Act, 1988
A CIP catalogue record for this book is available from the British Library

All rights reserved • ISBN 978-1-84869-837-6

Printed in China • LTP/1400/1992/1017

2 4 6 8 10 9 7 5 3 1

With your Paw in Mine

Jane Chapman

LITTLE TIGER

LONDON

From the moment she was born,
Miki loved to snuggle on Mama's tufty tummy.
"Mama, you are the plumpiest pillow in the
WHOLE ocean!" she sighed happily.

All around was cold sea and empty sky,
but Miki felt safe as the waves rocked her gently.

"Time for a swimming lesson!" smiled Mama.
"Let's fluff you up so you'll float when the big waves come."

Mama pawed Miki's fur till she was as puffy
as a pompom! Miki couldn't help wriggling.
"You TICKLE!" she giggled.

"Come on then, fuzzy," laughed Mama,
sliding her into the water.
"Put your paws in mine and
kick those feet!"

When it was lunchtime,
Mama rolled her pup over
and over in seaweed until
only Miki's paws stuck out.

"Roly poly pudding!" sang Mama.
"This will stop you drifting away
while I look for something to eat."
She gave Miki a kiss, then flicked
her tail and dived into the ocean.

Miki was snug in the kelp fronds, but she missed Mama.

A little way away was another furry parcel just like her.
"I wonder if that's an otter?" Miki thought,
paddling over to see.

"Er . . . hello!" she smiled shyly.
"I'm Miki. What's your name?"
    "I'm Amak," replied the parcel.
"I'm waiting for my mama,
    she's gone hunting."

"Me too!" said Miki. "Waiting is a bit lonely, isn't it?"
Amak nodded, so Miki splished a little closer.

"Let's wait for our mamas together," she suggested bravely.
"We could hold paws too . . . if you like."

Amak thought for a while. "I'd like that," he said.

From then on, Miki and Amak always
stayed close while their mamas
went hunting.

Miki taught Amak how to float
upside-down and wonder at
the feathery forest below.
 "Wow! Look, Miki!"
called Amak, as turtles
flew through the
water beneath
them.

At night, after fluffing up their fur,
the mamas and babies cuddled together.

Keeping hold of each other's paws, they slept peacefully
to the sound of the sea's soft lullaby.

One morning, while Miki and Amak were
splish-splashing and their mamas were away
hunting, the sky began to darken.

"Where has the sun gone?" asked Miki.
"And what's happened to the sea?"
     The blue-green waves had turned black
and white, and rain was falling all around.

"I don't like this, Miki," whispered Amak. "I'm scared!"
     Miki was scared too. She wanted Mama.

Suddenly a huge wave crashed and —SNAP!—
the seaweed tore beneath them!
Miki and Amak were pulled apart
in a whirl of sea, spray and sky.

"Amak! Amak, catch my paw!"
cried Miki above the wind.

Amak reached out, stretching
as far as he could . . .

. . . until the two pups were paw in paw on the
rumbling, tumbling tide.
"I'm glad you're here," shouted Miki.
"I feel safer with you!"

But then they heard other voices –
babies and mamas calling out over the water.

"Help!"

"This way!"

"Catch my paw!"

Miki and Amak were joined by more and more otters, all reaching out to catch hold.

The wind blew and waves crashed, but the raft of otters clung tightly together as the storm raged on.

And then, over the howling wind, Miki heard her favourite
voice in all the ocean calling her name.
"Mama!" she called back.

Mama swung Miki up for a snuggle.
"What a storm!" she whispered.

"I missed you, Mama," snuffled Miki.
"But Amak and I, we looked after each other!"

Mama smiled down at her brave pup, cuddling her tight
until the winds dropped, the waves softened and the
blue-green ocean was calm once more.

"We all need someone's paw to hold when the big waves come," smiled Mama.

"Well, I have your paw, and Amak's paw . . . and the paws of all our new friends," laughed Miki. **"We'll always have each other!"**